Copyright © 202

ASN Technol

1

CELEBRATING

MEDIOCRITY

SOME OF THIS HAPPENED

Contents

Backstory

I thought it'd take a couple of months.

A quarter, tops. It's been a year.

So far, no good. It should've been a routine, run-of-the-mill, pick-the-best-of-the-bunch sort of affair. It wasn't.

I've been balls deep in the "process" for a year.

Vying, wooing, Whatsapping, right-swiping, gas-lighting, sweet-talking. I've hired obsequious agents, reconnected with long-lost relatives, trotted the globe, fallen out of love, committed my birth-chart to memory, made a fool proof Excel questionnaire and even had a professional picture taken.

Nothing ventured, nothing gained right?

Bollocks.

I colossally overestimated my "demand" and comically underestimated the "supply".

As a solid-6 on the dateability index – bang-average height, dimpled-smile, curly coif (meticulously oiled each-night while fervently hoping the dormant bald-gene doesn't get expressed), early-30s, "non-vegetarian", upper-caste bloke – my chances were decent, at best. The eclectic background –schooled in Bangalore & London, fluent Hindi, passable Kannada and subtitled Marathi, an Irish passport, a stable-if-boring day job and an active-blogger by night – seemed to scare off more women than a glimpse of Shakti Kapoor's nipples (you've seen the picture).

Now, a year older, with a rounder-midsection, an inflation-beating salary bump, wispy streaks of grey in the 'fro and firmly ensconced in my mid-30s, I am teetering on the edge of premature unclehood.

Needless to say: I am #singleAF.

But being an insufferable optimist – I continue to reach for the stars. Must be the rollicking '70's RDB soundtracks I love, subliminally infecting me with the "do not settle for what's available, strive for what you want" bug. No vaccine for stupidity, eh? But screw it – I've decided to go big or go home.

I am a doer with get-up-and-go. A bit anal about organization and punctuality. A tad too eager about becoming a dad. Always on the charm offensive. Outgoing, flirtatious, unfiltered. Pushing boundaries, putting myself out-there, taking rejection in my stride and making things happen. Shoot first, apologise later. See, I am the guy who'd buy you a drink, make you laugh, charm your dad, and pre-emptively put our unconceived kids' names on the private school waiting list.

And yet, nobody is ringing my doorbell and asking me to marry them.

What follows in these pages are some escapades of my life that actually happened in my seemingly eternal pursuit of the purest of all our traditions: an arranged marriage.

Passivity is a bore. So, I am metaphorically squeezing into my LBD, flashing some thigh and like all self-aggrandized Dilwalas, going to find my Dulhaniya.

Prologue

36 hours into my water fast.

Window seat, sun-kissed and hurtling across space in a straight-line towards Namma Bengaluru. Clear-headed, lowered resting heart rate, comfortably reclined in the plush business-class seats. Fancy much?

Imbecilic child next to me hammering the screen with both his tiny fists. His mum, Chanel's finest oozing out of her every pore, looks on at him lovingly – her precocious little angel.

"Ha – isn't he a little devil", I say. Passive-aggressively of course.

"I know, he's got so much energy! Don't you cutiepie?".

Cutiepie is blowing perfectly spherical snot-bubbles now. Like those bubble-gum things, except misty green.

Mommy wipes his face, smile intact, and lets him continue his stress-test of Emirates' in-flight infotainment unit.

I excuse myself to go for a piss. These water-fasts means I take loo-breaks every hour. But then again, it's a day closer to my 10% body-fat target. You win some, you lose some. Delighted to point out that shuffling out of the window-seats into the aisle remains a demeaning experience, even in business class.

Time flies. Before we know it, we are taxiing on the Kempegowda tarmac.

****

"One and a half saar, it's very far. Won't happen return trip for me." The universal Automan's sales pitch. I let him get away with it though. It's back-breaking work.

"Okay banni…"

"Great saar."

Bright blue church pews double up as seats in this fine automobile. Like sitting on a park bench where two tectonic plates meet. The cushioning is threadbare. My bony arse feels every one of Bangalore's innumerable potholes along our one-hour trip. Automan bouncing on his seat like it's a pogo-stick, me gyrating on the church pew like I am on a sybian.

"Where coming from, saar?"

"Dublin...Ireland."

"Oh, UK na? Queen saar?"

No, and no. But leave it. Experience has taught me to only pick winnable fights.

"Yes. Close to Queen." Not quite 6-feet-under.

"Very good. Family in Bangalore saar?"

"Yes – here since the '90s."

"Very good, I am from Chamrajpet saar. Marriage aaita saar?"

Two minutes in and I've to get defensive.

"Not yet...looking to find someone."

"Oh, good luck saar. These days girls very difficult. Find someone simple. What caste?"

I used to think of myself as quite a direct guy. But that's based on my closeted Irish standards. Out here, everyone cuts to the chase. Saves everyone time. Why bother with perceived niceties?

"Maratha...", I muster wishing he'd see through the lukewarm response.

"Very good. Upper caste aaramse you'll get. Very fair girls."

Melanin, or the lack of it, dictates everything here. Your diet, your mate, your job, your house, your self-worth.

"Saar, you speak Kannada or Marathi?"

"Both, but mainly English..."

"Then very easy saar, don't worry."

I lean back on the church pew; arms spread across the seat. Like I used to as a nubile, young fella back in the day. Let the smells and sounds of my city overpower me. The honking, the pandemonium, the deafening two-stroke lawn-mower engine. It was great to be back.

Automan pulled into stop at a red light, a nanosecond after it turned green. Turned off the engine, put his feet on the handle, lit a beedi and watched the clock count down from a whopping 180 seconds. Cars, vans, trucks, bikes, cycles all around us. A thriving, heaving sea of metal, diesel, noise, and humanity. I didn't know I missed this. I absentmindedly stared at a feral cow crossing the street, its enormous udders swaying, people patting its back. It proceeded to drop a gigantic green turd-cake on the road. And nobody batted an eyelid. Life just...carried on.

"My daughter no marry saar. She's already too old, will be difficult to find for her."

"Oh, is it...how old is she?"

"26. Getting very late. I try everywhere, no boys only. Everyone wants working girl."

I was 35. Damn. I had no chance.

"I don't mind any girl – working or not working…."

"No no no no, can't give to you. Different caste alva saar."

I didn't have the energy to correct Automan that I wasn't interested in marrying his daughter. Not until I see her at least. But his use of the word "give" made me wince.

"Which caste are you looking to get your daughter married into?"

"Local caste. Kannada-speaking. Anyone is fine in our caste saar."

"What about some other guy that your daughter likes?"

"No problem saar. If no Muslim, we are okay saar."

So desperate dad wants to give his ancient 26-year-old daughter to anyone that she likes if it's not a Muslim. Why not?

17

"Why not?"

"Cultural clash saar, very different peoples."

Part-time Automan, full-time Anthropologist.

"What age do you think is too old to get married?", I ask, fervently praying I am not older than Automan's filters.

"26-27 max, after that no babies."

"Okay. And what about for men?"

"Saar, we are ready anytime." Looking at me in the rear-view mirror, slapping his thigh and laughing deliriously.

Was Chamrajpet's Jordan Peterson onto something though? Didn't I think I was too old? Wasn't I looking for someone who'd make a great wife and a better mother? Didn't I also want someone who'd be a snug cultural fit?

Automan voices his truths while I stifle mine, lest they become real. This is a man who knows exactly what he wants. There's something to be said for that – I am just not sure what.

* *

The smell of carbs welcomes me home.

The unmistakable sizzle of butter on the underside of a dosa. Mom is already banging them out by the dozen. Cooking for your firstborn never seems like a chore, eh? I wish I could give this much unconditional care to somebody, some day.

She's a petite, energetic, vociferous, caring lady. Steadfast, principled but not immune to bouts of mild bigotry. Acing a double-barrelled MA (French) and MBA (Economics), getting hitched to my dad at the ripe, old age of 29 and raising two healthy, functional, psychologically balanced kids. She is, to me, the archetypal modern Indian woman. #WifeMaterial.

"Your hair looks like a beggar's. Get it cut."

Indians and cutting to the chase.

"Mom, it's fine – I want to grow it out."

"If you grow it out, I'll throw you out. Get it cut, look decent, you've to meet so many girls. You are middle-aged as it is…"

"Girls like the salt-and-pepper look these days, ma."

"Yeah, I don't like such girls."

Yep. She doesn't.

Dad, surveying me above his unfurled newspaper, chips in.

"Are you still keeping up with the carnivore diet?"

"Yeah. But I also fast now."

"Fast?"

"Yeah, I don't eat for days sometimes."

I can only see the back of my mom's head when I said that, but I am 99% sure she's scowling.

"And that's good for you?"

"Yup. Eating is much more dangerous than not eating. You should try it out."

"Hmmm. Send me some videos on this."

Ever the sceptic. Dad's always been a keen reader, a sharp talker, a staunch ally, and an excellent friend. Mr Dependable. And the first person I turn to whenever trouble befalls me. Which is often.

We devour the dosas, sitting at the same dining table we've sat on for decades. Gossiping, laughing, talking. And then, the inevitable question comes up.

Mom ventures first.

"We've looked at so many girls. Relatives, friends, matrimonial agents, sites. We can't find anyone suitable yet...what type do you want?"

Like I was buying an iPhone.

"Mom...it's hard to paint a picture exactly. Most of the girls I am attracted to, don't want me. Most that are attracted to me, I don't want..."

"Yeah – but like, what characteristics are we supposed to search for? You want a book reader, na? And someone qualified? And who speaks Kannada?"

Check. Check. Check.

Whom did I want? Short version: a woman with a big brain, a bigger heart, and an even bigger derriere. Long version: …

"Mom. As far as I can tell, three things. Physical attraction. Intellectual compatibility. Loving family."

"What is this intellectual compatibility? Your dad and I had no intellectual compatibility."

Dad nods along.

"I just mean that we watch the same shows, read the same books…".

"You can just tell her what to watch and read."

Why didn't I think of that?

"Yeah, but I don't want her to be obsessed with low-brow nonsense. Like Reality TV or wanting a pre-wedding shoot or talking in Hinglish or Kinglish or whatever."

"What rubbish. You are obsessed with Bollywood too."

I am. More on this later.

"You forced us to watch Sanjay Dutt movies in Gandhi class at Swagath theatre on a Wednesday. And you are talking about intellectual compatibility?"

"Mom, that was when I was 16. People change, they mature…and I did that ironically. I write about Bollywood as an intellectual exercise, I love the razzmatazz, but I take it with a pinch of salt. I just mean I want someone with some depth."

"Compatibility, depth…what rubbish. If she had any depth, why would she marry you?"

Dad chimes in with an excellent point.

"Anyway, we have six biodatas shortlisted. Meet them, talk about whatever you need to, and just pick one."

Biodata sounds like a medical profile. It's essentially a match's CV: her name, height, weight, skin tone, caste, relatives' maiden names, job, salary, an "about me" (which no one, including the writer, ever reads), a couple of photos in varying outfits (a "traditional", a "modern", a "PG-13 but hot"), birthday, birthdate, birthtime (for horoscope matching reasons), three sentences on the type of man she's after, and all relevant personal and professional contact numbers, social media handles and I kid you not, a LinkedIn profile.

My parents had scoured through thousands of these in the last few years. They had filtered out the chaff and presented me with six. They'd be on-board if I married any of them.

Arranged marriage is like Tinder if its algorithm was powered by your mom. Carefully handpicked, rigorously researched, and whittled down to the chosen few. Like a buffet with your favourite starters. Of which you pick one. And eat it for all eternity.

"Fine, I'll meet them. That's why I am here anyway."

As opposed to lying semi-horizontally in my Lazy Boy guiding Arsenal to Champions League glory on FIFA back home.

Monday: Can You Smell What's Cooking?

"Bangalore's Oldest Pub" screams the neon sign. In electric blue. I push the doors marked "Pull" and step inside, the sticky beer-stained floors welcoming me home. It was about 2PM and the place was already heaving. The unmistakable odour of deodorant, sweat, and beer.

I see the back of her head, first. Queueing up for the loo. Why does the ladies' have interminable queues everywhere in the world? Anyway, I digress. She's about 5'2 (check), luscious black hair, Adidas Superstar trainers and the slightest hint of a tramp-stamp when she raises her arms over her head to stretch. Triple check.

Conversation time, me thinks. Nothing ventured...

"Shame there's only one toilet, right?". Excellent start. Pub ergonomics. Guaranteed to send any woman into a tizzy.

"Hahaha yeah…" Plays with her hair. Like all girls do. Perfectly pierced nose, kajal-eyes, thin mouth, tiny mole on her forehead. An open, disarming, tired smile. But a smile, nonetheless.

"You know you could just use the men's?". Knowing perfectly well that there's no way she'd do that.

"No…I don't think so". Extra enunciation on "think". This was a Bangalore hudugi for sure.

"I was just joking…"

Ms Monday shrugs. Signalling nonchalance.

"Nice to meet you! Did you have a good flight?"

"Same here, thanks! And yeah, it was as nondescript as possible. And thankfully no masks needed or anything."

"Oh, is it? I hope you wore one anyway?"

Er…why?

"Yeah, I did. Can never be too safe you know".

It's not a lie if it's for a good cause, right?

"That's good. I haven't caught the virus in two years and don't want to catch it now!"

Ms Monday seems to have mistaken me for a contagion.

"Don't worry – I am vaccinated and boosted. You won't be catching it from me!".

"Okay…".

Not convinced. Wouldn't blame her, to be fair.

"I'll go grab a table. Would you like me to get you a drink?"

"Yes please, a bottle of Budweiser. Leave the top on, I'll take it off when I drink it. See you in a bit!".

I take her extremely specific drink instruction to the bar, grab her bottle and get myself a pint of the house tap, pick the first table I see and sit in the chair, facing out towards the bar.

First impressions? Easy on the eyes but her drink choice OCD and general aura of depraved cleanliness had me on edge. I let it slide – maybe she's just being extra cautious.

She takes a solid 10-minutes. Her pee-break takes longer than my shower. Make a mental note to keep an eye on the soaring energy-costs when we get married. She steps out, beaming smile in-place and sits down opposite me. I wish I could remember if I stood up and pulled the chair for her, just assume that I did.

"So, finally! Nice to meet you again. You are not as tall as I imagined!".

Ouch. Indians and cutting to the chase.

"I left my stilettos back in Dublin," I say with a grin.

I get the laugh. All good.

"So, how's your #groomhunt going?"

"Hahaha it's alright. Nothing fancy. I guess it'll happen when it happens."

"Fair enough. I just like to make it happen."

"But these things are complicated..."

"True – anything worth doing is though, right?". Confucius in the house, ladies.

"Yeah – my parents have given me a deadline. But yeah – it'll happen when it happens."

"Cheers to that!", I say holding up my glass.

Ms Monday proceeds to unscrew the top, whip out an industrial box of tissues, wipes the rim, and finally clinks my glass in my outstretched hand. Uh oh. Alarm bells.

"Wow. That's quite the forensic routine. Do you do that for every beer?"

"Yes. I am a bit of a clean freak; I am very careful about what goes into my body!".

Fair enough. I couldn't be more different though. I am extremely careless about what goes in, or out, of my body.

"So, tell me about yourself...", Ms Monday asks.

"Well, you've read my biodata, right?". Ms M nods.

"I guess there's more to me than what I can fit into three sentences. But as a one-liner: I am easy-going, ambitious, single, and looking to change that. What about you?"

"Nice! And you plan on living in Europe forever?"

"Yes."

"I've always imagined myself living abroad, you know? That's what attracted me to your profile in the first place."

"And not my charming smile?"

Blank face.

"I don't go only by looks…"

That explains why she agreed to meet me then. I guess she means she prefers the whole package, whatever that is.

"Really? I do go by looks. If I didn't find you attractive, I wouldn't be here in the first place."

Ms Monday furrows her brows.

"That's really shallow though…"

"Oh yeah, totally is! I mean that physical attractiveness, subjective as it is, is my first "filter". If I don't like what I see, I am not interested in pursuing it further."

"But that's objectification…!".

"How so?". I am genuinely curious.

"You only like a girl for what she looks like."

"No, I didn't say that. I said that I only meet a girl to get to know her after I find her attractive. It's not that I'll fall for the first attractive girl I see. It's the first barrier-to-entry, if you will. Only after that I do I look for emotional, intellectual compatibility…".

"Wow. That's almost misogynistic."

Um, what? Why?

"Why?", I ask, genuinely curious.

"Because looks fade. And if in thirty years' time you don't find me attractive, you'll leave."

"Is that misogyny or is that just…. life?"

"I want someone who'll stay by me no matter what I look like in the future."

"That sounds like an insurance policy."

"It's what marriage is."

"Bloody hell", I say in my faux-Ron Weasley voice.

"I mean, it's a patriarchal institution designed to keep women enslaved in the kitchen."

Gosh. Is it? I thought it was somewhat more romantic than enslavement.

"So…why do you want to get married?", I ask exploratorily, tactfully trying not to tip Ms M over the edge.

"Because society wants me to."

"And you don't?"

"Obviously I do…!"

"But why?"

"So I can have a partner for life, travel, have someone to come home to…"

"Then society wanting you to be married is irrelevant."

"I wouldn't get married if society didn't want me to. I'd just live with a partner!".

"Umm…so why don't you do that now?"

"Because my parents want me to be married."

"So let me get this straight: you want the perks of marriage without being married because marriage is enslavement. What you'd really like is to live with somebody, but you are reluctantly agreeing to get married to keep your folks, and by extension, "society", happy?"

"Sort of. And that I don't think any relationship should be based on looks."

"Don't lionesses choose the lion with the best mane as their partner?", I ask proud at my razor-sharp wit.

"Lionesses don't get married either.", Ms M says blunting my razor.

"Touché." She had a point. "I meant physical attraction is innate in all living beings. And is totally subjective. And I think it's okay for anybody to have any kind of filters for their potential partners."

"Look, all I am saying is that men are shallow. Looks aren't everything."

"Want to hear my theory on this?"

"Sure…". Leans back in her chair and looks around the now deafening pub, already up to her ears with my incessant questioning.

"I reckon men choose partners on looks, women choose partners for stability."

"So, women can't be stable without men?"

"Again, I don't mean that. I mean if a man had to choose between a pretty girl with issues or…"

"Why does the girl always have issues?"

I don't know about womankind, but I know one girl who might.

"It's not always – it's just in my example."

"Pick a less offensive example!".

"Umm… I am trying to make a point."

"If your point hinges on the pretext that a woman has issues, your worldview will continue to remain male-centric."

Right. That sounds like the final nail in the coffin of my non-existent anthropology career. I change tact.

"Okay, never mind. My bad. Let's talk about something else?"

"Only because you know I am right!"

"Yes. You are. Agreed. On a lighter note, tell me what's your favourite thing to eat?".

"Hmmm. I love all kinds of food. But I go crazy for Italian."

"Nice! I had the best pasta in Sicily on my last holiday. And I don't even like pasta."

"What! Pasta is gorgeous!"

"I guess, I mean…it's alright. Do you make it yourself?"

"No way – Swiggy baby, that's where all the action is at. I don't cook much."

"Oh okay. Must be expensive though? How do you afford takeout every day? And why do you not cook?"

"Umm…have you ever spoken to a woman before?"

"Not as often as I'd like to…. what do you mean?"

"Firstly, Swiggy isn't that expensive. I work extremely hard and make a lot of cash. I can afford whatever I want, especially gorgeous pasta on demand. And the opportunity-cost of cooking is far too high. I'd rather outsource the cooking and spend my valuable time doing things I enjoy."

"Like…what?"

"Catch-up with friends, Netflix, shop…you know, the usual."

"Okay…"

"You know we'd never be having this conversation if I were a man."

"I guess not. Unless there's a gay version of Shaadi.com."

"I mean you wouldn't ask me if I cooked if I was a guy."

"Why not?"

"You are only asking me this because you want your future wife to cook!"

"I sure hope that my future wife would cook." No word of a lie there. Would anyone want to be with anyone who didn't cook?

The waiter chose this precise moment to drop in and ask for our order. And I decided to tap into the apparent wisdom of the crowds.

"Sir, does your wife cook?"

"Excuse me…?", asks the waiter, two-parts taken aback and one-part up for a chat.

"Does your wife cook?"

"Sir, I am trying to get married for over 6 years…". I hear the angst in his dialogue delivery. Poor sod.

"Oh wow. Okay, no worries. Thanks, and good luck. We'd just like another round of the same please. Bottle top screwed on, as usual."

And then I add, "Would you want your wife to cook?"

"Sir…of course." Knew it!

"Okay, thanks!"

Waiter zooms away, leaving me alone with Ms M again.

"Okay – that was just embarrassing! I can't believe you did that!". I am beginning to cop on that Ms M finds most things unbelievable.

"Um...talk to the waiter?"

"Yeah, about such private things!"

"Okay, it's literally just a conversation about his wife."

"Look, this may be normal in Finland, not here."

"Do you mean Ireland?"

"Whatever land. Look, this isn't going to work. I agreed to meet you cause you appeared to have a more progressive mindset; you are just as misogynistic as the waiter." Ouch. Poor lad didn't stand a chance out here.

"Umm...okay. No hard feelings! Can I just ask, have you ever met a man who according to you wasn't a misogynist?".

"Yes! It's rare as hell but am sure he's out there somewhere."

"I am sure he is too. Good luck on your search."

And just like that, I only had five matches to choose from.

****

Namma Metro was surprisingly quiet on the way back home, softening my aversion to public transport. The lashing rain didn't help. I managed to find a still-warm seat (seat warmth is revoltingly intimate, but I digress), throw my head back against the smudgy glass window, close my eyes, fold my legs, and try to get some sleep.

The 20-minute walk home shouldn't have been stressful. Until the pack of unruly dogs, who terrorised me when I was 6 and still terrorise me now, decided to chase me all the way back to my doorstep.

Mom opens the door before I finish panting.

"Well! That was quick! Shall we start printing the invitation cards?"

It's impossible for me to know if she was taking the piss.

"How was she? Tell me everything!".

"Mom, wait…". My lung-capacity wasn't what it was. I was sucking in more air than my defunct Hoover.

"So…yeah, not going to happen with her."

"Why not! Wasn't she pretty?"

"She was. She got offended when I indirectly told her that."

"What? You must've made a stupid joke."

"I made many, ma. But she just…I don't think she wants to get married. Or maybe she does, but it must be on her terms, and I am not the right kind of guy for her."

"But why not? How long did you talk for? Do you want me to call her folks and ask?"

Indians and cutting to the chase.

"What! No, please don't. She's a bit strong for my liking."

"You only wanted intellectual compatibility, right?"

"But we aren't intellectually compatible."

"Why not? Doesn't she watch and read what you like?"

"We didn't even talk about that."

"Then what did you guys talk about? How do you know she isn't right for you?"

"Mom…she has fixed ideas on how the world works. I don't think she's going to change her mind on it easily. And I really don't want to spend the rest of my life trying to get her to see things my way."

"This is why I kept telling you to get married when you were in your 20s. Girls after 30 will not listen to anybody, not their parents, and definitely not you."

She might be right, you know.

"Mom, I was too young then. I barely knew myself."

"What have you achieved knowing yourself now? You must get off your high horse and pick someone fast! All my friends are grannies now and I am still raising a man-child."

"Mom…give it a rest. Half of those grandkids don't have both sets of parents."

"Yeah, true…anyway, shall we put her on the long-list?"

Like I was consulting on an M&A project.

"Nope, no point. Let's move on and see what the others are like."

"Your dad and I thought she was the best one!"

Oh boy. We are all deluded. And then it dawned upon me – I could quite easily console my mom on my lack of choice.

"Mom, she has a tattoo on her back…"

"Oh, leave it then. We'll see what the others are like."

Ka-ching.

****

Bed beckoned.

Monday turned out to be a failure, but like all failures, it taught me something. I must pull my punches a bit. Be a little less adversarial. I am equal parts stubborn and deluded, to be fair. Maybe I needed a reality check.

Maybe I was a misogynist.

But my conscience felt fine. I didn't think I had overstepped my mark, nor that my questions were too intrusive. Or that my expectations were too lofty. Or that my chat with the waiter was infringing Ms M's privacy.

I wasn't single for a lack of effort or desire. Maybe I am just unlucky? I reckon I need to double-down on what I am, start afresh, and go after it again. Luck turns, after all. And all I need is one girl to like me. Or at least, not vehemently hate me.

Either way, there's always tomorrow.

Tuesday: Million Dollar Baby

Another day, another dollar.

Shit, shower, shave, solve, sell: the morning routine of champions. Except mine ends after shave - I am on holiday for Christ's sake. I only "solve" and "sell" when on company time. Although this hasn't felt like much of a holiday so far. Arranged marriage dating is a full-time gig. With no perks. And no salary. But allegedly the eventual reward is the big pay-off – a lifetime of sanguine happiness.

Maybe the juice is worth the squeeze. We'll see.

I am hit with a barrage of questions as I roll out of bed and head to the war room. Or kitchen, as most of you know it.

"She was the best one, what did you manage to not like about her?", Dad with the opening remarks.

"She's great, you guys did a great job shortlisting her! Looks nice, but just not my type. To be honest, I'd bring nothing of value to her life." Swift, succinct rebuttal. Classic firefighting: credit their effort, showcase my shortcomings, leave enough room for silence, drink a cup of tea.

"Fine. Are you meeting the next girl today?". Works every time.

"Yes dad. I was thinking I'll do it right now – morning date, sunny day, and plate of idli-vada."

"Okay, good. You want me to drop you?".

"Dad, I am not going to school. I'll just walk it."

"Walk? It's like five kilometres away. In this heat, and traffic! You won't survive."

Dad always thinks walking anywhere in Bangalore is slightly more dangerous than facing enemy-fire head on.

"It's fine. I've to hit my 10k steps today. I'll get an auto back. Plus, I need some Vitamin D."

"Okay good luck. And don't get argumentative with her."

"Noted. I'll keep it simple. You know I don't go looking for a fight! I generally keep an open mind…"

"Yeah, but people don't like being questioned! They feel threatened by it!"

"Why?"

See what I did there?

"Because most people are insecure about themselves, and what they think they are about. And your questioning puts them on the spot."

"But I need to know what someone is like before marrying them, right?"

"I didn't know what your mom was like…"

"Maybe you just got lucky then?"

Sidebar: moms are always within earshot. You could be on the dark side of the moon and mention her, and she'd hear you crystal clear. Mine was no different.

"We both got lucky, we found each other, and then we worked on our incompatibilities. Nobody is perfect, you must make it work."

"Mom, I completely agree. This is what I want too. I am just saying, forget about any intellectual compatibility or whatever, I just want to marry someone with whom I can at least negotiate with. Somebody who's willing to introspect, encourage an alternative perspective, think for herself, instead of having a rock-solid perception of how the world works. I mean, her perception could be right, but I still wouldn't want that."

"I doubt you'll ever get married." Dad cutting to the chase, as usual.

"There's bound to be someone like that, right. Who also matches all your filters?"

"Yes – but we are short on time. You are nearly 40!"

"Better late than never. Better good and slow, than fast and wrong. Better right first time, than wrong many. Better get going."

■■

"So…you are flying to London today?" I ask, desperately sticking to the obvious.

Ms Tuesday sat across me in the finest Adigas establishment in all of Jayanagar. Steaming idlis fog up my glasses, as I unfurl a balled-up tissue from my pocket to wipe them. It manages to do the job somewhat. I now had streaks of tissue paper debris across my glasses. Classy.

"No – I plan to jump out somewhere over Baghdad."

Nice. She gets it. I smile. She smiles. Ka-ching.

Ms T: A Cambridge-educated, globe-trotting, matcha-tea drinking lawyer. She's squeezing in a daytime-date with yours truly, enroute to the airport to board her flight back to London. She aims to work on the plane, bang out a few emails, cab it to Shoreditch, and get back home by 2AM. Sheesh. Our romantic getaways are going to be....an experience.

"You've certainly packed light then!"

"Hahaha yeah – these baggage rules are so...ugh!" Ms T makes a face somewhere between missing a last-minute penalty and inhaling a noxious fart. Adorable. This one was a looker.

"I know right? I am flying back home after a year cause my mum has lined up these girls for me to meet. Like some sort of swayamvar. So, I didn't pack that much, most of my good stuff is at home." Just slyly putting that out there – testing waters. Telling her I am "available". And interested.

"Oh wow! How's that going then?"

"Well so-so. You win some, you lose some."

"Yeah well, same here. Where are the suitable men!" Shakes both her fists at an imaginary heaven, smile still intact.

My idli was now soggy. (Not a euphemism). I dunk it in the delicious sambar and do what my dad told me not to: I asked a pointed question.

"So, what is your type then?"

"Somebody ambitious, successful, driven...I'd hate to be the alpha in the relationship, you know. I want somebody who'll compete with me, push me in my career as I will push him in his, a mutually beneficial relationship built on solid compatibility and growth."

I let that percolate. Maybe she's hiring a VP for her firm, and some of the job-spec has subconsciously drifted into her answer.

"You must have come across many that tick those boxes?", I ask inquisitively.

"Only on the surface. After a couple of conversations, it all just falls flat. They all seem content, comfortable in where they are. Which is great for them, but like I said, I want someone with actual drive."

Gosh. I'd be lying if I said I wasn't at least a little intimidated.

"Yeah, I guess we are simple creatures. And I totally hear you – far too many are comfortable with ordinariness…"

"Exactly. What's the point of life otherwise? And marriage, specifically? We both need to enhance each other's lives!"

"Does the "enhancement" have to be purely professional though?"

"What do you mean?"

"I mean, there's more to life than professional glory. It's a job, after all. I'd rather my wife enhanced my life in other ways – strong emotional support, someone who laughs at my jokes, is a loving mother to our kids…."

"Most people have jobs. I have a successful career!"

So, she stopped listening after that sentence. It's amazing how people always hear what they want to hear. Including me. Time for the next negotiation tactic: mirroring.

"You have a successful career?", I say in my most neutral, inquisitive, soothing, non-judgemental voice.

"Yeah, I lead a high-performing team, I am the go-to girl for all my clients, I bring in millions in revenue, and I worked my ass off to get to this position."

"Wow. You are a high achiever!"

"I don't like to brag about it obviously, but I am. I guess that's why I wouldn't want to give any of it up and take a backseat with someone who wasn't at least equally driven."

Fair enough. I would reluctantly be the househusband and work on my business and writing if it meant that we had a happy, healthy, loving marriage. I guess I wouldn't view it as a "sacrifice", as much as being a unified team. My professional achievements aren't the only source of my happiness and confidence.

"I hear you. You know what you want, and that's great. What do you do when you aren't working?"

"I am at a senior position, which means long-hours and lots of responsibilities. I love what I do, and honestly, it doesn't even feel like work. It keeps me engaged!"

So, no hobbies then. Okay. There must be something that she loves doing outside of her job. Another red flag: she hasn't asked me a single question. Yet.

"Damn. You love what you do! You know what I do, right?"

"Yeah, you run a consultancy business, I think. How's that going?"

"It's alright. Pays the bills. I don't live to work. Or even work to live. I guess I value my autonomy and time more than working for someone. I am privileged enough to use my time to earn the money I need. It's never enough, obviously. But at least I love it. And I spend the rest of my time dabbling with things I love – writing, talking, travelling, family."

"I see. You rather do many things well, than one thing excellently."

"I guess so. If I have a good time doing them."

"I see myself growing with my firm, dedicating my best years to it, acing life! Nothing gives me more joy!"

"What about being a mother?" Sorry dad.

"Excuse me…?"

"I mean, that would give you more joy I imagine?"

"Would you enjoy being a dad?"

"Yes! I'd love that! I love responsibility, I think I'd be quite hands-on, and I am eager to have my own family."

"Hmmm. But kids are such a chore! And they are expensive little time-stealers!"

"Um, I don't think you'd feel that your own child is stealing your time."

"I would. I just...don't like that idea of being tied-down or slowed-down by anyone."

"Except your employer."

"My employer pays my bills! Kids are all take-take-take...And isn't the world overpopulated anyway?"

"Is it?"

"Yeah! 8 billion and counting. Why do we need more of us?"

By that logic, the best thing we could do for the planet is to kill ourselves. Don't worry dad, I won't say it.

"I think the bigger problem is that the planet is underpopulated, not overpopulated. For the first time in history, people under the age of 30 have fewer kids than ever before."

"Easy for you to say! Walk around Bangalore and tell me we don't have enough people."

"Population isn't the same as population density. Anyway, why is the world's problem your problem?"

"Because it's by changing ourselves that we change the world."

"You'd like to change the world?"

"Yes! In my own way. Wouldn't you?"

"I'd like to change my world."

"Huh?"

"Make my world better. Happier, fun, warm...you know, things that kids bring. I think everyone changing their own worlds should eventually make the world better. Or not."

"Kids! Plural! How many kids do you want?"

"I am too egotistical to not pass on my genes. I'd like as many as possible! Rather have and not want, than want and not have. The pain of regret is so much worse than the joy of responsibility."

"Wow. Are you serious? With climate change, overpopulation, dwindling resources...you want to have multiple kids?"

I was being berated for not caring about efficient resource utilization by a woman with three packed suitcases, a dress costing four-figures, the latest MacBook, and a whiff of Dior's top-shelf perfume.

My idli was past soggy now.

"I guess it's natural to have kids and to perpetuate life. It's the human-centric approach. And I genuinely believe the point of life is to take on responsibility. To embrace discomfort. And kids bring that, and more."

"Ok boomer."

Fair enough. In my defence, I am yet to meet a 50-year-old living alone in their 2-bed apartment that they bought on a 30-year mortgage thanks to their excellent employer, looking back on their life and patting themselves on the back saying "Yeah, I did this right."

"Why have kids when you can adopt? There are millions of potential-responsibilities for you take on!"

"True, there are. I guess if we couldn't have our own kids that's a viable option."

"That's so selfish! Wanting your own kids. If you really loved kids, you'd just adopt!"

"So, you mean you aren't against kids, you are just against having any of your own?"

"I just don't think kids are a priority for me right now. Focussing on my career, yes. Finding a compatible husband, yes. Kids will happen if and when they happen."

"Sure yeah, I agree. I don't want to have kids tomorrow. I just mean I'd like to have kids in the future, once my partner and I are on the same page. I mean that not wanting kids at all is my dealbreaker."

"That's such a weird dealbreaker to have! You can't decide to reject a potential match because they aren't ready for kids immediately."

"But being on the same page on this is vital, right? It'd be a bit late to find out we want different things three years into the marriage."

"You make this sound like a contractual obligation."

As opposed to Ms T's job-spec for a husband. But okay, maybe I am being too business-like.

"You know what I reckon. If there was no such thing as the biological clock, I don't think this discussion would even be necessary. And yeah, it's unfair that the clock runs out at the cost of your career. But I don't think it's either kids or career, surely. Employers understand that and they are quite accommodating. I mean, I am the product of working parents, and I've turned out okayish. It's possible, and it's not easy. But it can, and in my estimation, should, be done."

"Am sorry, but this is just luddite thinking. You've heard of freezing eggs? IVF? There are so many tools for the job now! You don't have to be hamstrung by the old-school method."

I already have the perfect tools for the job the last time I checked. I mean, I get it. Ms T was talking sense, and I am looking for a life-partner not a baby-producing machine.

"Point taken. Expensive options, emotionally taxing and stressful, but valid. I still think they are wonderful technological advancements but useful as a back-up when the main system malfunctions."

"So is a car. Why don't you walk everywhere, like we were meant to? Just because it's unnatural doesn't make it wrong."

"Okay. Just cause it's available doesn't mean it needs to be used."

"Ah. What's it with you guys these days? Would you be as eager if you had to go through 9-months of pain? And that's for a single kid – you want many!"

"I'd like to think that I would. Luckily for me, I don't have to put my money where my mouth is."

"Wow. Entitled and misogynistic. You are quite the catch."

Uh oh. I'd done it again. At least it wasn't that long a walk back home.

■■■

No Namma Metro this time.

Just a long 5km walk home whilst slaloming between motorcyclists and cratered pavements. Pausing, reflecting, playing it back in my head. Two women of their own accord think I am a misogynist.

Both couldn't be wrong, could they?

But why is my conscience unmoved? Why do I feel that I am not crossing any taboo lines despite two random women and my parents telling me I am? What am I missing?

My dealbreakers are too strict, probably. I am stuck with an elitist, entitled, toxic masculinity that reeks. Being myself isn't working.

And I still can't get to wholeheartedly agree with Ms T's take. To each their own, right? If she's right, I am not the guy for her. If she's wrong, I am still not the guy for her. Logically, the only thing that matters then is if we are right for each other. And my conscience doesn't allow me to say that we are.

No unruly dogs chased me home tonight – my circuitous thoughts did that job tonight.

I glance across at the old pan-shop my friends and I used to sneak out and smoke at. It's the same dude running it. Over fifteen years. He looks exactly like how I remember him. He probably wouldn't recognise me now. I spend another few minutes' staring into my past-life before I realise what I was doing: buying time before I break my parents' heart again.

Screw it, time to face the music.

****

"What was wrong with this one, then?", mom welcomes me home.

"Not much, to be fair. I don't think she wants to have kids." A succinct summary am sure you'd agree with.

"What? Why not?"

"They are resource heavy..."

"Are you listening to this?", mom yells across the room to my dad.

"Yeah, I am. Go on...", he yells back.

"So yeah, apparently they are time stealers...", I continue.

"But she's already 33!"

"And her best is yet to come, at least for her employer."

Mom looks on in disbelief. Surely, there's more to this?

"Surely there's more to this?", she asks, right on cue.

"I guess she isn't ready for kids, nor is she worried about the biological clock."

"Do you want me to ask her parents?"

"What? No! What would you ask? Why doesn't you daughter want to have kids? I am sure they'll be delighted to answer that."

"But this is so unnatural...", mom says. Still in disbelief.

"She did say she's open to other...routes. Adoption, IVF, etc."

"Okay, forget it. You can't change her mind."

"Exactly."

"So, she's off the longlist then?", dad asks.

"Yep. Struck off."

"Okay. Next one tomorrow?"

Like a conveyor belt in a factory.

"Yeah, next one tomorrow."

At least the debrief wasn't as bad as I feared it would be. Every cloud, and all that.

I collapse on the couch and pick up a book. Read it on autopilot until it's bedtime.

Wednesday: Baby Carrots Also Scream For Their Mothers

I arrived early, as usual. A full ten minutes. And already, the warning signs were all there: plush seating, menus with an embroidered hardcover, waiters in three-piece suits in the sweltering heat, copiously high 3-figures on the right-hand side of the menu, a proper country-club crowd with well-mannered children, and dulcet classical music piping in through tiny-but-expensive-and-loud speakers.

I'd give anything to be in a dingy highway Dhaba. Luscious Chicken 65 and butter naan on my mind.

But Ms Wednesday chose this joint specifically. She even rang and booked ahead. Fine. At least she's proactive and organized. That's a good start. I need to be more accepting. Get a grip, man.

I make idle chat with the waiter who walks me to the table.

"Hello Sir. Would you like to look at the menu while you wait?"

I already had, so I ask him what he'd recommend.

"Sir…"

"Please don't call me Sir, anything is fine."

"Okay Sir, I mean okay. Our most popular dish is the Cashew Mozzarella Mockmeat pasta. I'd also recommend the chilli garlic potatoes to start."

"Ah okay. Do you have any Chicken 65?"

The waiter looked at me like I just auctioned his firstborn on eBay.

"Sir…we are a Vegan restaurant."

Everything went deathly quiet.

So quiet I could hear next table's knife grating against the ceramic plate. A gentle, dull, faraway sound that nestled in my brain. The same brain which was still trying to process this new information. Slowly, it began to make sense – the clientele, the ambience, the prices...

"I'll wait for my...friend to arrive."

"Sure, no problem. Bottle of Vegan water, sir?"

I should've left it. But...

"How is the water vegan?"

"It's the filtration process. We don't use isinglass as it's made from fish-bladder."

Isinglass? Isn't that what that sword in Game of Thrones was made of?

"Okay, I'll have a bottle please."

I want to taste the lack of fish bladder.

Waiter nods, turns smartly, and disappears behind the ostentatious curtains. I go back to talking to myself, trying to assess the situation. Ms W surely isn't vegan, is she? She wouldn't have made it through my parents' iron-clad filtration process. Was she a recent convert? Did my folks

70

just miss it? Maybe she's vegetarian, which is less militant but equally problematic. Maybe she chose this place ironically. Maybe like me, she's a raging carnivore and this is an elaborate practical joke.

My mental decision-tree was cut short with the arrival of Ms W.

First impressions: tall. I mean, taller than me I reckon. Curly hair. Wooden frame spectacles. Zero makeup. No discernible smile. Probably preoccupied. I have direct line-of-sight to the clock behind her head which just struck 8PM. Right on time. Ms W, in all her glory.

"Hello!", I say. Holding out my hand. "Nice to meet you."

She shakes it, says hello in a voice that I wasn't expecting. A tall-girl with a short-girl voice. I am not sure if that makes any sense. Anyway, no biggie.

"So, you found the place then?", she says. Finally smiling. Opening with a question. She's already bettered Ms T. Even showcasing concern. This is good.

"Yup, all good! I've never been here before. It's um…. nice," I lie.

"Oh really! Loads of NRIs come here. It's really packed normally, that's why I booked a table."

"Ah okay. It does seem to be priced for NRIs!"

"Yeah, all the ingredients are locally sourced, no additives, everything is pure, organic, and classy. I guess they must charge high to maintain their margins."

They sure do. The fish-less water was 200 rupees.

"So…how has your trip been so far?", Ms W with the opening gambit.

"It's been quite hectic. But nice to catch up with my family."

"That's nice. Is your sister here too?"

"No, she's back home in Ireland. She's working on her PhD thesis, so no time for fun."

"Oh wow! She must be smart!"

"She is. She got the brains, and I got the looks."

Ms W laughs. Not bad. This might work.

"And what do you do?", I ask. I had a vague recollection that she was a freelance content-creator or such like.

"So, I am a freelance writer, editor, and producer of podcasts and videos for high-end, green brands."

Green-brands. Uh oh. Is that what I think it is?

"That sounds awesome! I dabble in content creation myself…"

"Oh, I don't like to identify as a content creator. That just belittles what I do – I don't create fluff pieces, or funny cat videos, or anything like that. I have a focussed, serious message that I like to pass on to the world. I'd do it even if I wasn't getting any clicks!"

"And what message is that…?"

Every fibre of my being knows what the message is. But I wanted confirmation.

"Hello ma'am. Are you ready to order?"

The waiter with impeccable timing. Suspense delayed for a little bit more.

"Yes – I'd like to start with the chilli garlic potatoes, please. And a bottled water. What about you?", Ms W didn't need to even look at the menu. She must be a regular. And two bottled waters? My ancestors are turning in their grave.

"I...already got a bottle of water. We can share that right?", I ask meekly. My voice betraying my thriftiness.

"No, I'd like my own one. What would you like to eat?"

That's that then.

What would I like to eat? I'd really destroy a lamb biryani. But not now. Not in here.

"I'll er...try the grilled tofu to start."

Ms W looks at me admiringly. My conscience tells me I've let myself down. But screw it. It's just one meal! I could find joy in it, somehow.

"Thanks. I'll bring it out to you shortly.", says the departing waiter. Already counting the day-on-day revenue growth, I bet.

"So, you know, I've met so many guys now that I have a readymade checklist of items that I ask them about.", says Ms W. Organized and self-aware. And she knows what she wants. I am curious.

"Okay...that's interesting. Do you want to give me a quick run-down?"

"Of course. It won't be quick, but I'll tell you my filters. And then quiz you on each."

Let the interview begin.

"Fair enough. What are your filters?"

"I'll keep it high-level for now – kids, pets, virtues and diet."

"Okay – that all sounds reasonable. What's my first question?".

"Pick the topic first, and I'll ask you."

"Okay…kids?".

Recency bias kicking in bigtime.

"I'd like to have at least 2 kids. What about you?"

Okay – that's an improvement.

"Yeah, on board with that. 2 minimum!"

Ms W smiles and does an air-tick with her extra-long fingers. I must get used to the height-thing.

"Okay, normally that wipes out 50% of the men most of the time. At least you are through to the next round."

"Really? Half of the guys you met didn't want to have children?"

"Yes. It's bizarre. They see them as a financial drain."

Tell me about it, sister.

"Yeah, I don't see them as that. Good we agree on it then. Next?"

"Next...."

"Are each of these dealbreakers by the way?"

"Yes. I want total agreement on each of my filters! These are super important to me."

"Okay, fair enough. I like that. I've been accused of being too shallow and choosy, but I like that you have clear boundaries and know exactly what you want." True statement.

"Good! So next...pets!"

"Go on...what are your questions?"

"Easy one first – are you for or against pets?"

Genuinely, I couldn't care less either way. I've never been big on pets. I've never craved for one. Can I picture myself with a Labrador? Taking it for long walks along the pristine Irish coast? To build my Instagram following, sure. But every day? No thanks. My approach to pets is the same as my approach to visiting the zoo: I like seeing animals on demand, not to be at my side constantly. I suspect Ms W loves it. But then again, maybe she's anti-pets. Maybe it goes against her morals. She wants to know where I stand without her biasing my opinion in any way. Smart.

"I am neither for nor against them. I haven't had any, but I've played with several."

Balanced. Not giving away too much. Not picking a side. Sitting firmly on the fence.

"I see…."

Does she? Let me ask.

"What about you?"

"I've always wanted pets – dogs specifically. Preferably like a rescue-pup or two! It'd be so nice to have them wandering about the house, taking them for a walk, having them play with the kids. It's how I always pictured my life."

Okay – at least she's honest and upfront. She likes dogs. Plural. But that's alright. Who doesn't? Maybe I can get used to having a furry friend. And maybe I can negotiate with her to do all the dog keeping duties. At least until I get the hang of it. I mean, she's going to marry a stranger, move to a different continent, and start her life over from scratch. The least I can do to keep her happy is get a dog. Or two. Right?

"That's cute! Like I said, I am indifferent either way, but if you are happy to take the lead on being the dog-mommy, I'd be happy enough to support that. And am sure I'll get to like the furry fella over time."

"Hahaha okay! That's good! It won't be straightaway obviously, and I'll train you as much as I train the dog."

"I might need more training."

Ms W laughs. Okay. So, I've made it this far into unchartered territory. I feel like Columbus stepping on hitherto undiscovered American soil. And just I was going to make another obviously witty remark, the waiter swoops down with the first course of the local, fresh produce. And two bottles of water.

"Here you go guys. Bon Appetit!"

I look at my tofu. And then at the chilli potatoes. They look tasty enough. The waiter serves us a serving of each with practiced flourish and proceeds to open the bottles. I ask him to only open one. Just in case.

I am no water connoisseur, and have the palette of a child, but I can tell you that the water tastes the same as any other water I've drank.

Anyway, Bon Appetit.

"I'll be back in a few for your main course order", the waiter says and waltzes away.

"So...tuck in?", says Ms W. "You've made it to the next round!"

"Woohoo. So, two more dealbreakers to go?"

"Yes – virtues and diet."

"Okay.... let me think."

Seriously. Let me think. I've no idea what she means by "virtues", but I sure as hell can blag about it enough so it vaguely sounds like what she wants to hear. I do that for a living, so I am not too worried about that one. But I know the diet is a real dealbreaker for me. If she's a vegan, and I still don't know if she is, it could complicate things. But I am willing to concede that there could still be a way to make it work. Maybe she wasn't a militant vegan and wouldn't mind me eating whatever I want. I could just about work with that. Yes, dinner dates and home cooked meals are going to be insufferably dull, for life. But at least I can cook and eat what I want by myself. Right? I mean, I do that anyway today.

I decided to leave the "diet" topic for the end. Let's dig into this "virtue" one for now.

"Okay...virtues.", I said, mostly confidently.

"Okay...who do you think the planet is for?", Ms W asks nonchalantly between mouthfuls.

Uh oh. This is precarious territory. This is going to get extremely political extremely quickly. And I'll say the right things now, only to get married to a hippie. And my kids will be Marxists. Or am I overthinking this? I mean, I could marry a Communist Hippie and life can still be great. Right?

"How do you mean exactly?", I ask. Maybe I misunderstood the question. Maybe I want to misunderstand the question.

"I mean...are you a capitalist?"

There it is. And yes, I bloody am. It's the only way to be that works. I do enjoy competition, growth, hard work, persistence, rewards, money. And I don't think it makes me a bad person.

"I guess I like the idea of making ends meet, and living a happy, healthy life."

Pathetic. Do I really want to get married more than I want to remain a capitalist? I don't know. Should I bother mansplaining Capitalism, and its virtues to Ms W? It's not going to be easy. Why is this arranged-marriage conversation anyway? I need to prep better for next time. If there is a next time.

"Okay. So, you are caring and considerate and view sustainability as the way forward?"

Am I? Do I? Isn't one bottled water more sustainable?

"Yes."

"Okay...we'll see about that as we go on, I guess."

Ominous.

And now for the inevitable...

"Last dealbreaker: diet. What are your food habits?"

Where's the waiter when you need him?

"I eat one meal a day."

"Oh wow." Ms W was impressed. This is uber-sustainable. "As you've probably guessed, I am Vegan."

So, the gloves are finally off. At least I made it past the appetizer this time.

"Okay…", I say in my least-judgy voice.

"I have been a Vegan for over three years, and it's changed my life."

I bet it has.

"So, do you eat meat?"

I eat only meat.

"Yeah, a bit."

Pathetic.

"Oh. Do you eat it often?"

Every day.

"You know, sometimes."

"Do you cook it?"

No, I just sink my teeth into a cow.

"Yeah, I do...I am excellent at it."

Silence from Ms W. The waiter is probably fleecing some other table. At least the bottle of water is unopened.

"Would you cook it at home?"

As opposed to a car dealership.

"Yes, I would."

More silence from Ms W. I can see the cogwheels in her brain grinding. She knows I failed on the last dealbreaker, but then again, I am not a bad catch. She's weighing it up. Can she live with this meat-eating reprobate for the rest of her life?

"I need to think about this. I don't even let my parents cook meat in our house."

God rest their soul.

"Why Vegan, and not vegetarian?", I ask, trying to rescue this.

"Because it's inhumane to drink milk."

It's not. It's inhumane to extract milk from oats, almonds, soy…Never mind. This is not a fight I can win. But as long as she's fine with me cooking, and consuming milk, and animals that produce milk, this is still salvageable.

"Would you want your kids to be Vegan?", I ask. Surely, babies need milk.

"Of course. We don't need dairy in our diet."

Yes, we do. Never mind.

"And I presume you don't want your husband to cook or eat meat?"

"I don't know. It's unfair of me. But I guess I'd be okay with it if he did that in a separate kitchen."

Wow. One wife. Two kitchens. Millennial marriages are truly pathbreaking.

"Separate dishes too?", I ask half-jokingly.

"Yes, of course. That's why I didn't share your bottled water."

Okay. I've negotiated enough with myself. Time to get real. I am a pet-indifferent, capitalist, carnivore. She's a pet-loving, left-leaning, Vegan. Romeo and Juliet had better odds. And they also had love. I had a four-question interview and a bottle of unopened fish-less water. That I am going to return at the counter on my way out. Soon.

"I see. Well, I don't think separate kitchens is an option. We might as well have separate kitchen in separate houses in separate countries."

"Why don't you try going vegan for a while? You'll love it!"

So, this is what the rest of my life would be like. Judgements, guilt-trips, and malnourished kids.

"Because I don't want to deny myself of a healthy lifestyle."

"Vegan is as healthy as you can get!", Ms W says indignantly.

Okay. And I am a Booker prize winning author.

"I am sure it is. I'd rather be unhealthy and happy. And I couldn't do it for all my life."

The waiter looks over to us, preparing to come over for the main-course order. There won't be one, mate.

"Thanks for your time anyway, I don't think this would be sustainable." See what I did there? "And I wish you the best!"

"Thanks! But just try it out once, you'll thank me later!"

"Of course. See you!"

Whew. Some progress, I guess? But not much. At least I didn't get called a misogynist. And I now have another filter to update my search with. I start trudging back towards Namma Metro.

Three down, three to go. It's darkest before dawn, and all that.

The unmistakable smell of ever so slightly burnt ghee hit me just as I was about to get into the metro station. I turn around, frantically looking for the source.

"Royal Darbar A/C Family Restaurant– Non-Veg"

I smiled.

I'd really destroy a lamb biryani now.

****

"Vegan", I say sheepishly.

"But so what, da? Just go with it, and then change your story. I told my wife that I picked up smoking after we got married. Too late now.", my childhood friend, over a few pints, in the same dingy pub we've been drinking in over a decade and a half. Stone's throw from Royal Darbar.

"That's false advertising."

"She's not going to go to consumer court."

"It's the principle. I just wouldn't be comfortable with it."

"With lying to your wife? What else do you think happens in a marriage?"

"With my repressed angst. That's a one-way ticket to anxiety town."

"You think too much man, wouldn't you have gone ahead if she wasn't a Vegan?"

Would I? Probably. I am deep into "any port in a storm" territory.

"I am not sure…it's a dealbreaker."

"You have new dealbreakers every day. You need dealmakers."

"I am not looking to filter anybody out. I am bending over backwards to filter them in."

"Like an overweight yogi."

"Touché. It's your round."

Two more ice cold pints arrive. I tap my watch to clear my dues. Down the last pint. Get the last metro back home. Sleep like the dead.

Thursday: Not Taking A Risk Is The Biggest Risk

"I feel she's not your type.", mom in the pre-breakfast KANBAN.

"Why so?", I ask. Moms know best.

"I can't put my finger on it. Something about her seems off."

Thanks for the clarity mom.

"I might as well meet her and see how things go. Nothing ventured, nothing gained."

"Oho! Where was this attitude ten years ago when you could've had the pick of the best?"

"Better late than never, right?"

"Fine. Am just glad you are finally taking this seriously."

"He's reached the other end of the spectrum now. He's being too serious.", dad's astute observation. "Maybe make a decision after a couple of meetings instead of cramming it all in the first one?"

"Dad, I've told you this before. My strategy is simple: reject fast, accept slow. No point prolonging the inevitable. Plus, I've to fly back on Sunday. I don't have any more holidays left for the year."

"I think you are doing too much on the first meeting. It's too intense."

"Oh, come on. It's not a billion-dollar negotiation. There isn't any stress. It's a basic conversation, that's all. We can handle it."

"You've done a great job so far."

Roll my eyes.

"What's her background then?", I ask no one in particular. "So... I don't waste anytime asking her."

"27, Bangalore born-and-bred, decent family, talkative, assists her dad in the family business…", my mom with the photographic memory.

"Okay. And why don't you like her?"

"I didn't say that. I just have a feeling you won't make a good match."

"Okay…we'll see. Any minefields that I need to steer clear of?"

"I remember speaking to her once, on a WhatsApp call. Ages ago. She has a strong Marathi accent.", my dad said. "Don't let that throw you off."

"Okay. I won't. That's fine. Anything else?"

"She'll say pain, when she meets pen.", my dad elaborated, while raising one of his eyebrows and seemingly questioning me. "You sure that isn't one of your dealbreakers?"

"Stop making out like I am being superficial. The accent is fine. I'll get used to it. It's not a dealbreaker."

"How will she manage in Dublin with that accent?", mom asks. "She'll be insecure about it always."

"That's for her to deal with, and I'll support her. She can pick it up over time anyway. You guys manage to be coherent when you are in Dublin, so am sure she can too."

"But we don't say pain when we mean pen."

Fair enough.

"If everything else is fine, and I like her, I won't reject her because she can't say pen."

I have committed now. It could've been my get-out clause. I just wasted it. Amateur.

****

Just a cup of tea this time. I've learned. Meal-dates are too ambitious. I have had three so far, and barely eaten once. A hot beverage is the perfect length of time. Long enough to get the formalities and dealbreakers out of the way, short enough to keep the novelty high.

Easier on the budget too.

Ms Thursday is late. It's fine. Fewer judgements. More slack. Take it easy.

As is now customary, I make chit-chat with the waiter. A rotund (no judgement) lady of about 40.

"Menu, sir?"

"Thanks. Just a tea is fine."

"Boiled, sir?"

"Yes please."

"Two minutes sir."

"Take your time, no rush. How's the business going?"

"It's good...many customers now. Business doing good!"

"Awesome! Are you the owner?"

"Yes. My husband and I are, we are in business for more than 10 years."

"Wow! And does he work here too?"

"Not today, he's on kids-duty today. Needs to drop and pick them up from school."

"Oh nice. Do you have many kids?"

"Yes, four!"

"Wow! And you manage to run a cafe too?"

"Yes – it's hard work but we can manage it. I have a good staff and my husband is hands-on with everything. Anyway, I'll get your tea shortly."

"Thanks!"

Wasn't that a happy little story. It's bog-standard. Mrs Rotund (no judgement) isn't in the minority. Guys like me are. With entitled lofty standards, blue-sky thinking, and grandiose thoughts of compatibility. Mr and Mrs Rotund have their problems too, am sure. But they don't seem to be lacking for action. They take challenges in their stride, under-promise, and over-deliver. They aren't shy of embracing discomfort. They make the most of whatever situation they are in. They get on with it.

I reckon this is what Indian parents mean when they ask us unmarried losers to "compromise".

I wonder if Mr Rotund even knows what his wife's favourite colour is. Or if it matters. Or if their "vibes" match. I am beginning to think successful marriages take the "fake it till you make it" approach: commit to a stranger you have vaguely positive feelings about in an overblown, expensive ceremony with everyone watching, wing it for a couple of years, and by then, everything works out. Then put your kids through the same rigmarole.

Ms Thursday's arrival puts a stop to my existential reasoning.

Petite, streaked hair, a former-braces-wearer-smile (#IYKYK), oversized Wayfarers, and a confident, almost authoritative gait.

"Sorry I am late. Traffic you know…"

I immediately realise what dad meant about the accent. It's…prominent.

"That's alright, I didn't have anything else going on."

Which sounds passive-aggressive, but I really didn't mean it to be.

Ms T doesn't catch the perceived slight. Thankfully. Clicks her finger in the general direction of an overworked Mrs Rotund and beckons her to our table with her finger. Strike 1.

"Yes ma'am. I'll be there in two minutes.", says the harried Mrs Rotund from across the floor.

Ms T nods authoritatively. As if she was extending her tolerance for tardiness on this occasion. So, being the righteous dweeb that I am, I decide to pull Ms T up on her own tardiness. But of course, being a simp, I do it in a passive-aggressive way.

"So…traffic too heavy, eh?" On a Thursday afternoon. In Bangalore.

"Yeah, my Uber driver was horrible."

Uber? I specifically chose this place cause it's like a ten-minute walk from Ms T's house.

"Why didn't you just walk?"

Ms T's face resembles mine when someone tries to explain String Theory to me.

"Because of the sun. And why walk when I can get a cab!"

"So, you aren't stuck in traffic, I guess?"

Here's the thing: people don't like when someone else points out the bleeding obvious. It's a visceral reaction. An assault on their ego. It never goes down well.

"This is India, man. People don't walk."

That's my fact for the day. In other news…

"Okay. I get it. I just walk everywhere; I find it quite convenient."

"Really? Don't you have a car? Oh god, I can't survive without one!"

"No, I do, I just meant for like little errands. And yeah totally, I couldn't survive without my car either."

"Thank God. I wouldn't ever marry someone without a car! I need a man to drive me around."

Ms T had a very Uber-centric vision for life. Maybe she's just trying to be funny. I laugh anyway.

"Of course. If you don't mind driving the kids to school", I say. Hilarious.

"Oh, I don't drive! It's not for me. And abroad, the rules and all that are so crap man. Like no way am I going to waste my time trying to learn. You have Uber there, na?"

Ms T definitely had a very Uber-centric vision for life.

"We have similar apps, yes."

"That's great then. Do you know if I can transfer my Uber balance from here or do I have to create a new account?"

Um…why would I know that?

"Um…I am not sure. You could speak to customer ca…"

"Oh god. So annoying. I am not going to waste my time with that. It's fine. I'll just create a new account."

Okay. Can we move on from Uber.

"Yeah, you'll be fine with a new account. Have you travelled abroad much…?"

"Yeah, I was in Germany for my MBA. Hated it! I loved my college life here during my English MA."

"Why?"

"The food, the language, the people…just everyone is so stuck up. And like I had to do everything myself! I was homesick within a week!"

"Oh wow. That sounds terrible! Where were you?"

"Berlin. It was just so bleh...I could've just stayed in Bangalore. It's so chill here man."

"Yeah, I like Bangalore too."

"Yeah, it's like the best city in the world! So happening!"

More facts.

"I mean, it's fun sure. Every place is different though, right? Has its own charm..."

"Arre what charm! Berlin is so boring dude. There's nothing to do."

"Okay, fair enough. Maybe it just wasn't your thing..."

"Naah, I love it here more. I've so many friends here too, so many things to do..."

"Nice. What do you like to do around town?"

"Meet up with my friends, go to the pubs, so much culture man...and the music scene is unreal here!"

My music-scene was listening to Kishore Kumar on the treadmill.

"So, you like going out then?"

"Yeah! I just feel so alive here...everyone told me Berlin was a party city, there are a few spots but honestly, I enjoy Bangalore much more. I don't know why anyone would leave here."

"But aren't you open to the idea of living in Ireland?"

"I mean, yeah. For a while, sure. Make some extra cash and come back!"

Hmmm. Ireland is home for me. As much as Bangalore is. I do an 80/20 split between the two currently. Maybe I could do a 50/50? I could work from home. It'd be a shame to leave my world behind. But isn't that what I was expecting of Ms T? Or any future wife?

"Yeah, I guess. It's not a terrible option. Do you know much about Ireland?"

"Not really. It'll be better than Berlin, am sure!"

"I mean, it's different…"

Mrs Rotund cuts me short as she asks what we'd like to have.

"Another tea for me, please."

"I'll get a cappuccino.", says Ms T.

Mrs Rotund nods and smiles and heads in.

"I mean, it's different…", I continue. "The culture is quite unique, and the people are lovely. Social, friendly, funny…"

"What's there to do?"

That's too open a question for me to answer.

"What would you like to do? What do you spend your time doing when you aren't working?"

"I told you na – I like meeting up with friends."

"To what end?"

"Eh?"

"As in, what do these meetings entail?"

"Dude...what's entail. Who talks like that! Also, I didn't know you had a weird accent! Are you like a proper NRI?"

"I...guess so..."

"See, I want a proper Indian guy okay. Not some foreigner. Those guys are so boring. They read books and stuff, and even their jokes are lame."

Mom knows best.

"Okay...what did you like about my profile?", I ask trying to change tact.

"You seem like an independent guy living abroad. I thought you'd be into partying and travel and stuff."

Interesting use of the past tense there. And I did like travel and stuff. Partying...not so much.

"You had a photo of you in some rooftop bar, I love such places! Would love to go there", Ms T continued. "And you are Indian right, so you'd have the right culture and values too."

I think Ms T uses "culture" to mean literally anything.

"Like what culture, do you mean?"

"You know...respecting women, respecting our nation, our values...Even though you live abroad, I feel you have those things."

That word 'nation' feels so jarring.

"I respect all nat..er..countries."

"Yeah, me too. But I feel ours is the best, the quality of life is so awesome here."

"If you can afford it, sure."

"No seriously! It's amazing. I can get a coffee for like 100 bucks. And I can get a maid, and a driver, and a cook. Like it's so convenient. That never happens abroad."

Probably because of enforced labour laws. But I digress...

"Okay. I am confused – you liked my profile because I live abroad, but you love life in India more?

"See, basically I want a guy who's Indian at heart but living abroad and who'll come back to India to live after a few years because I like life here better."

"What's an Indian at heart?"

"Like I mean, you know…normal."

"Elucidate please?"

"What?"

"Describe what you mean by normal?"

"Dude, it's obvious. Like a normal Indian guy."

"But normal is subjective."

"I don't know what that means…why do you talk so weirdly?"

This was a washout. I am at my wit's end trying to understand what Ms T is looking for. Lemme try again. I'll take it back to basics.

"Okay. Hang on. Lemme back up a bit. What did you like about living in Berlin?"

"Nothing."

"Did you make any German friends?"

"Just casually. The way they talk is so funny."

Ms T could literally be skin deep.

"Fair enough. What makes you think you'd like life in Ireland?"

"Arre, if it's just for a few years, I can adjust na. Like I did in Berlin"

"But what would you do during those years?"

"Shop, travel, party...."

I am trying not to grind my teeth.

"But do you have a goal, or a vision, for our life together?"

"See, I don't overthink so much. I just live in the moment."

"Won't you get bored? Liked you did in Berlin? You must have some hobbies, right?"

"I like watching movies."

Okay – that's promising. I love movies too.

"Okay – what's the best movie you've watched recently"

"Bhool Bhulaiyya 2."

No comment.

Mrs Rotund brings us the coffee. I want to neck it and walk out. But wait. Ms T is just…simple. That's not the worst. She can learn. Attitude more than aptitude, right?

Ms T rips three brown sugar sachets with her teeth. Dunks it in her cappuccino. Strike 2.

"What's one thing about you that you'd like to change?", I ask like a desi Dr Phil.

"Umm…I wish I was taller."

"Okay, I meant something that you could change."

Without breaking the laws of physics.

"Oh…I want to get into politics."

Where did that come from?

"You can do that any time. It's in your control.", I supportively say.

"Are you a political person?", Ms T asks.

"No."

"Oh. But you watch the news, na. It's so interesting what's happening in our country."

I need to steer this conversation into something tangible. One last push.

"I don't watch the news at all."

"Arre…you should. How will you know about your country if you don't watch? Our leaders are putting in so much work to improve our nation."

"Okay."

This was fast becoming a party-political broadcast. I need to take evasive action.

"Why do you want to get ma…"

"You know, we will soon be a bigger economy that UK and USA combined. You should set up your business here."

Mrs Rotund thankfully breaks up Ms T's sales pitch to clear the coffee. She stops dead in her tracks while walking away from our table as Ms T clicks her fingers again. She turns and walks back towards us, seemingly mesmerised by Ms T's beckoning index finger.

Strike three.

"Yes ma'am? Anything else?"

"Dessert menu."

Please? I say in my head.

"Yes ma'am, two minutes."

"Actually, no need for that. Just the bill would be fine, thanks.", I say officially kicking off Operation Cut My Losses and Get Back Home.

Mrs Rotund nods and smiles and heads her merry way.

"I think we are quite different...", I start, turning to Ms T.

"Yes, don't think this will work."

"Exactly. Thanks for your time, and good luck. I am going to head to the metro station!"

"Arre why baba, I'll get you an Uber."

****

Namma Metro was the emptiest I had seen all week. As was my list of remaining options.

Ms T was just...I mean, we weren't just on different pages. We were on different books in different languages in different countries separated by copious space and eternal time. As I sat there staring out of the still grubby train windows, watching South Bangalore whooshing past, I realised I wasn't disappointed, or sad, or guilty. I wasn't even angry. Or frustrated.

I was feeling sorry. For people coasting through life bereft of purpose. For denying themselves the full splendour of life's experiences. For passively accepting things as they unfold. For not thinking for themselves. For not challenging the status quo. For not embracing uncertainty. For not risking failure. For fearing discomfort. For blindly pursuing inanity.

South Bangalore kept whooshing past. Time kept ticking. People got off the train, more got on. Everything just carried on. As it always had. As it always will.

I see a 2-year-old jumping off the seats to try to latch on to the handlebar.

I know he won't even attempt it next year.

Friday: Mind Your (Family) Business

"Have you done all your packing? Make sure you take all your important stuff! Keys, wallets...", mom with the same question for the 96th time.

"Will do it tomorrow, ma. There isn't a lot to do. I'll have it done in ten minutes."

Packing is overrated. I'd happily dump all my clothes in a binbag and fire it vaguely West. I can't figure out why people fret about this stuff. It's like taking a day out to carefully arrange your groceries at the till, only to put them all in the fridge a few minutes later. There were more pressing matters at hand.

"When is your flight?"

"Sunday morning at 3AM."

"So, you'll need to be in the airport by midnight? Do you need a COVID test?", dad asks.

"Yes and no. I'll get the auto back." Automan would be delighted with my custom.

"Okay. Shall we start shortlisting some more girls?", mom asks.

I don't know. Honest answer. Maybe we need to revamp the process. Blow it up and start over.

"Let's see how it goes today and tomorrow.", I say. Cautiously optimistic.

"You should just do video calls from Dublin, don't have to fly down to see anyone until you at least make it past the first meeting.", mom says. "How much have we spent on flights?"

I knew to the third decimal point how much we had spent. The mood was already dour. No need to take it lower.

"Yeah, I'll do video calls first for the next batch."

"When are you going out today? I'll get all your clothes washed, and ironed, and pack them before you are back."

"Okay, thanks. I'll go early evening."

****

Ms Friday was in great spirits. Friday 4PM is the golden hour for the working class. I should know, it's the best I feel all week. Sunday nights are the worst. I had timed this right at least.

"You are so funny! Can't believe we didn't meet before", says a jovial Ms F. I knew I wasn't the sole source of her delight, but I'd take a compliment all day.

■■■

"Thanks! Only to look at, though."

More squeals of laughter.

I am such a sucker for easy attention. Pathetic, really.

"You know, I've been on the matrimonial apps for six years now. My account number is like 3 digits."

"Wow." Mine was six digits. Ms F has been single since Netscape Communicator. #IYKYK.

"That's forever! How come?", I ask. Mostly curious. Mostly to mentally prepare myself for six more years of this.

"Ah you know…the usual. Didn't find anyone I liked. I did have two engagements though, so that's some progress."

It is progress, right? Like how attempted murder begets the same punishment as actual murder.

"Damn. That must've been rough…"

"To be honest, I am glad neither worked out. The first one was a disaster, but the guy's family was loaded. So, my folks were pushing me hard for it."

No problem there. My family was loaded too. With debt.

"Okay…but you didn't like him?"

"Not really. He was alright. Like, I wouldn't look at him if I randomly chanced upon him on the street. But you know,

I'd have been fine. He had no sense of humour and was a total mama's boy. Two huge red flags."

"But you still went ahead with it?"

"Yeah, I was 29! I didn't exactly have much choice. He was the best of the rest."

Sheesh. How bad were the rest?

"Okay. So why did you break it off?"

"Way too many gory details! Don't want to ruin my Friday with that. The other guy was a lot sweeter!"

"Okay...but why did you break it off with him?"

"Because he was divorced, and conveniently forgot to mention it. And just before the day of the wedding, his parents wanted a huge sum of money."

And I thought I had it bad. At least all I had to deal with is conversations about separate kitchens and political allegiances.

"That's...crazy. How much did they want?"

119

Again, I am curious. What's a huge sum of money?

"A lot.", Ms F says. Terse. "And my dad was willing to pay it too. He just wants me gone."

"He'd pay someone off to take you?"

"Yes. Indian parents are the worst. Mine are even more so."

By now, dear reader, you'll know that I am not a fan of generalisations. And sweeping statements. I had to interject here.

"That's sad. Mine are great, and really supportive."

"The classic #NotAllMen excuse?"

Uh oh. Do not get dragged in.

"Yeah, well…"

"Indian parents are the worst. Trust me."

"If you say so."

Another round of beers. Happy Hour has truly set in.

Ms F leaves the table to find the washroom. There's bound to be a queue.

I fiddle around on Twitter as I wait. Liking, RT-ing, scrolling. Taking the cheap dopamine hits. Ms F, like the day she was named after, was fun, bright, and effusive. She'd been at this for long. Unlucky and a victim of circumstance. But it's not so much what happens to us as how we respond to it. How had Ms F responded?

I could just ask her cause she's back.

"Such a long queue to the washroom!", she says exasperatedly.

I know. I've written a chapter about this.

"Yeah, so...tell me. Are you Vegan?"

"Eh? What? No way. I eat anything that moves."

Tick.

"Do you think the world is overpopulated?"

"Um...I don't think so."

Tick.

Deep breath before the million-dollar question.

"Do you cook?"

"Yes, of course. It's a life skill. Like swimming."

Exactly. Like swimming. Tick.

"Is this your questionnaire for all girls?"

No, but I've learned from my recent past.

"Yes. I've had to tweak it in light of new information."

"Hahaha. Okay. Have you met a Vegan?"

"Briefly."

"What! In Bangalore?"

"Yeah…"

"I am so sorry!"

"Yeah, her loss!"

We clink our glasses. Cold beer on a hot afternoon. Hey Siri, define bliss.

So far, so good. No dealbreakers. Do I continue digging? Or just call it here, let things percolate, and come back for round 2. I do have a flight to catch though. Might as well make the most of it now.

"Tell me about your family", Ms F asks.

Oh wow. She's interested!

"We are a huge bunch, scattered all over India and abroad actually. But quite close knit. What about yours?"

"Oh, we are a typical nuclear family. Nothing exciting. I have an older brother living in the US, and a few cousins around Bangalore. I am not close with any of them. I like choosing my relationships!"

Fair enough. Minimal familial involvement then. I'll take that.

"I see. I am close to all my cousins; we have a tight group and get to see each other rarely. So, it's always fun when we meet."

"Okay. You do you!"

Interesting choice of phrase. I sense Ms F's detachment. Maybe resentment, even? I need to pick at this.

"You guys aren't close then? The two sides of your family, I mean?"

"Not really. We have our separate lives. And I can't be bothered with it all, honestly. I prefer having a small circle of close friends."

"But you are close to your parents?"

"Not really. My dad and I don't get on. All he cares about is getting me married off. My mom is busy doing stuff around the house all day. We only talk about how old I am, and why I can't get married."

"Am sure they'll be sad to see you go!"

"I wouldn't bet on it."

I don't need to get involved here. It's her life, her family, their dynamics. Not everyone needs to be like me. But her lack of empathy or interest in her own family is gnawing at me.

"You know, I can't wait to move out of home and start my own life with my husband…", Ms F offers.

It does sound great. And she certainly means it. But I am family man. Actually, I am an extended-family man. Family Man Pro Max.

"Have you always wanted to live abroad?"

"Not really, I am okay living anywhere as long as it's different to where I am now."

"You really don't like living with your folks, do you?"

"You wouldn't either! It's just…toxic. And it's easy for you – you live all alone and don't have to deal with all this emotional pressure."

True. But then again, it's not an us vs them situation. Although I can see how Ms F has convinced herself it is. Stress makes enemies out of friends. Prolonged stress makes your dad your nemesis. An echo-chamber of toxicity is hard to break out of. We romanticise escape, fetishize independence, and villainise family. Please take this with a bucket of salt – I am not a shrink.

"Yeah, I get what you mean. It can get quite suffocating..."

"Exactly. That's why I want somebody who's stable, independent, and with a sorted life. Not a mama's boy."

"Even though you got engaged to one."

"Because of family pressure. Not my choice."

"What exactly is a mama's boy?"

"Have you not seen some of the men here? They can't function without their mom. She does everything for them. They expect the same from their wives. Like a newer model to replace the older one."

I know guys like that. How much of this is nature versus nurture, though?

"I don't want a son, I'd like a husband.", Ms F continues. "Indian parents bring their sons up differently to their daughters. And even a grown man continues to give in to his mother's pressure. That's just…weak."

"It appears weak. But it's conditioning, right? It's hard to just flick a switch and become a new person after marriage."

"Oh, come on. It's the least a guy can do!"

Fair enough. I am beginning to understand I don't have the foggiest idea about how these dynamics work. Or are expected to work. Why do we have afterschool tuitions for 6-year-olds and nothing for Indian men primed for marriage? You'd think a basic toolkit would come in handy. Total addressable market – half a billion. I make a mental note to investigate this further.

"I want a guy who has the guts to do something his parents are against. For me."

Wow. That's a helluva ask.

"Why?"

"Because that shows that he prioritises me over anyone else. I'll happily go against my parents."

"But that's probably because you don't like them."

"So...?"

"It's easier to go against someone you don't like."

"But doesn't the guy like me?"

"Why can't he like you both?"

"No. He needs to draw strict boundaries!"

"Not in all cases."

"Is that another #NotAllMen excuse?"

"It's just reality. You don't have exclusive control of your husband's thoughts...he's still free to choose."

"I don't want exclusive control. I just want him to be strong against parental influence."

"Even if their influence is for the good?"

"It's never good. Don't you watch any shows? Or see it in your own extended family? In-laws make things worse."

Indian TV shows wouldn't be my first port of call for a treatise on familial dynamics. Nor would it be my extended family, to be honest.

"So, you wouldn't move into your husband's place after marriage to live with the in-laws?"

Just a hypothetical. Don't judge me.

"Of course not! Why do you think I even liked your profile?"

So again, not the charming smile.

"Why is that?"

"You live alone! And I imagine you'll want to live abroad for the foreseeable, with your partner and family, and no pesky in-laws."

"Yes, for the most part. I also fly my parents over to visit me, so we all get to spend some quality time together."

"How long do they stay for?"

Excuse me?

"It depends…"

"Like, are we talking days, weeks, months…years?"

"I don't have a schedule."

"Okay – we need a schedule. I don't want to live with my in-laws! That too in a foreign country. I'd rather just continue living where I am."

Ms F really hates her folks. Something is screwed up here.

"I am not going to have a schedule for when my folks can see me."

This isn't a prison. Or a hospital visit.

"This is what I mean – boundaries! You need to establish them."

"And there are also times when I'd want my family – wife, kids, and I – to spend time in India with my folks. And hers. They'd love that. I'd love it. What's to lose?"

"Oh my god! Are you serious? You should have said this sooner."

I wanted to make the most of the happy hour before the offer shuts.

"Do you just want someone to spend time with, look after your folks, and clean your house?"

"No. I'd like someone who does all that and more. Together. As a team. What else do we have to do?"

True story.

"Live on our own terms, travel, so many things!"

"But it's not one or the other. It's not a binary choice. You can always have the future you desire. You just envision it, and make it happen."

"I do. But I don't envision in-laws in any scenario."

"Wouldn't you want your folks to come over and visit us in Ireland?"

"Are you serious? Of course not. Why would I want that?"

"For the same reason I want mine to come over."

"No, your relationship with your folks is yours to deal with. Mine is mine. We don't need to keep everyone happy all the time. It's a never-ending task."

I don't want these silos.

"And you are sure that's the healthy way forward?"

"Yes. What you are advocating for is unhealthy. It's co-dependence. And a need for making others happy."

"Parents aren't others."

"Anybody who's not you are others."

"Including your husband?"

"Initially, yes. Over time, no."

"So maybe you'll warm up to the parents over time, too."

"No, I won't. This is a tried and tested formula that doesn't work. At least not in the Indian context. If you had Irish parents, it might have been different. But you don't!"

Sorry mom, dad. You should've been Irish, and you could've come over and stayed with us. Your fault.

Happy hour was nearly done, I reckon. As was my interest in Ms F.

"Fair enough. To each their own."

"Yeah, and next time, you need to make it explicitly clear on your profile that you expect your wife to welcome her in-laws. You'll stop wasting genuine people's time!"

"Understood. Any other profile improvement tips?"

"Yes. You are just another Indian mama's boy with a fancy passport. I'd make that your tagline."

Quite catchy, to be fair. Might get me some hits. I'll trial-tweet it and do a quick A/B test.

"Noted. Safe trip home. And thanks for your time."

∙∙

Ah well. It was good while it lasted. Ms F ticked most of the boxes, except one. A new one that I didn't know needed to be ticked. I now had a longer list of requirements, and a shorter list of suitable candidates. In 5 days. The inverse of what I was aiming for.

Glance at my watch. It's peak rush-hour. Which means Namma Metro would be jammers. I don't fancy rubbing up against a hairy armpit for two hours back home. I am going to be a spoilt brat and get an Uber.

One more to go then.

By my grasp of the process of elimination, she would be the one I end up marrying. That's how Bollywood movies end right? But not necessarily crappy novellas. I've surely seen it all by now. What fresh hell could tomorrow possibly bring?

I can't wait to find out.

I get home, say goodnight, and hit the bed.

Once more unto the breach, folks.

Saturday: It Was Written In The Stars

"Don't forget to pack your passport!"

"Yes ma!"

I've been traveling back and forth for 17 years. And still this.

"Why did you decide to meet so late? It's already 8PM! Will you be back by midnight? You need to be at the airport three hours before your flight!"

"I know, I know. I'll make it, don't worry!"

"Hurry up and go. You sure you've packed everything?"

"Yes!"

"Okay good luck! See you later!"

****

Going for dinner today. The full shebang. Who knows when I'll get authentic butter naan and butter chicken next. Might as well make hay while the sun shines.

Proper Punjabi Dhaba. Outskirts of town. Shorts and T-shirt weather. Mosquitoes already having their fill on my shins. I get a sweet and salty lassi as I wait for Ms S to turn up. I don't like the sweet-lassi. I find the salty one too one-dimensional. So, I mix it up. So, sue me.

Slap the irritating suckers with on my shins with one hand, scroll Twitter on the other. Nothing new to report.

Ms S turns up in 4-inch heels, a handbag straight out of Vogue, and a billion-watt smile. Eases into the chair, shakes my hand, and says she is delighted to see me. Not a bad start.

Open, honest, direct, feminine.

Saved the best for the last, perhaps?

"Nice to meet you too!", I say. I genuinely was. Ms S feels like a breath of fresh air, radiating warmth and optimism.

And an indescribable coyness. Like she had just committed some mischief that nobody had cottoned on to.

"I am sure! I am quite the catch after all!", Ms S flirtatiously says. Even bats her eyelids.

"Yeah well, you certainly know how to make an impression!"

"Hahaha thanks! You know, no word of a lie, this is my first-ever arranged marriage date!"

Oh boy. Lemme think – is that good or bad? Pros: no preconceived notions, blank slate, no baggage, and seemingly here on her own accord. So, definitely interested in getting married. Cons: she has nothing to compare me against and will probably look to play the field for longer.

On balance, it is what it is. Make hay while the sun shines.

"Well, in that case, I am glad to be your first. And possibly last."

"Hahaha. We'll see. Stranger things have happened."

They sure have.

"So what made you to want to go the arranged marriage route?", Ms S asks. Razor eyes on me and her switchblade smile intact.

"Because I am open to all avenues of…possibilities. The ends justify the means, right? All roads lead to Rome…"

"Rome being a lifelong, loving relationship?"

"A solid goal, I think?"

Ms S nods profusely.

"That's the thing with dating around. The end goal isn't immediately obvious.", she says. "With this approach, at least we both know exactly what's on offer. No dilly-dallying!".

"Yeah, I agree. It's open, above-board, and there aren't as many guessing-games to contend with."

"Yup! Do you mind if I just order a lassi too actually? It looks delicious."

"Sure, no problem.", I catch the waiter's eye and he's over in a flash. It's like my coolest moment of the trip so far. I mean, it's a low bar. But I'll celebrate the small wins.

"Yes sir?", waiter asks.

"One sweet and salty lassi please", Ms S says. Nice choice.

Waiter nods and heads off.

"Nice choice. Most people go for the sweet."

"I know, right? I find the sweet one too sweet. And the salty one is too…boring."

A woman after my own heart.

"So anyway, like I was saying…", Ms S says without missing a beat. "I want to get married, I want to have my own family, I want both sets of parents to be on board, and I'd like to do that soon. The arranged marriage route is probably the most optimal."

"Check. Check. Check. Check. And check.", I say. Utterly original.

Waiter's back with the sweet & salty lassi. Frothy at the top, with a pink and white stripey straw. I ask him for the menu, although I am quite sure what I want.

"Shall we get a Chicken 65?", says Ms S.

A woman after my own heart.

"Yes! And maybe the Gobi Manchurian too? They'll douse it with that MSG thing. It'll be delish."

"Oh my god – yes please!"

So, we ask for exactly that.

"So tell me then...straight off the bat: what are your biggest dealbreakers?", Ms S asks.

"Okay, I wasn't sure of what they were before this trip. But I have a better idea now..."

"Go on..."

"I am quite sure I am not a misogynist, and I am fairly certain I am not a feminist. So, first dealbreaker, anyone who's too much on either end of the spectrum would be a dealbreaker."

"Okay…that's reasonable. You aren't a wifebeater are you?"

"Only on Tuesdays."

We both laugh about domestic violence. Political correctness gone mad.

"Okay. Next dealbreaker?"

"Wait – let's do one each. Your go."

"Okay…I've to think. You have much more practice than I do!".

"That's your fault for being too slow."

"True…okay, I can't be with a workaholic."

The waiter interrupts our quiz with piping hot plates of Chicken 65 and Gobi Manchurian. I can smell the MSG from my seat. Gorgeous. The wisps of steam make it totally instragrammable.

"This looks amazing. Am going to tuck in", says a visually excited Ms S.

I didn't hold back either.

"So anyway, I can't be with a workaholic. Just whatever, there's more to life than boring Excel…", says Ms S between mouthfuls of steamy chicken.

"Okay, that's fair enough. I am on board with that."

The waiter comes back with a plate full of quintessential Indian salad – couple of chopped onions and a pyramid of lime.

"Next! Your turn!"

"I can't marry a vegan."

Ms S bursts out laughing.

"Okay, I can't either. That's just…weird."

"Yep. Your turn."

"I am close to my parents, so I want to be with somebody who respects that and treats them like he treats his own."

"Yeah, that's a given. I am on board with that too."

What's going on? Is this a con? How is Ms S saying things that I want? Or am I just hearing what I want?

"You'd be okay with leaving them and moving to a different country?", I ask. "Hypothetically, of course", I add hastily.

"Yes of course! I know what I must do, and that's completely fine by me and them. I do want to start my own life and have my family and live a fulfilling life. I'd love if they could come visit us of course!".

Wow. Shiver me timbers.

"Oh, and I absolutely love Ireland. The scenery, the accent, the culture, the poets...I think you already knew that though.", Ms S presses ahead.

The hits just keep on coming.

"Right. Are you sure you haven't been paid to say this?"

"Huh?"

"Never mind. It's just...I haven't met anyone who said what you just said."

"About Ireland? It's a tiny country...not many Indians know anything about it!"

"No, not just that. The other things too."

"Okay. Maybe you've just been hanging out with the wrong crowd."

"You can say that again."

"Sir, main course?", the waiter asks.

"Butter chicken...?", Ms S asks quizzically.

You've got to be kidding me.

■■

Siri reminds me that I need to leave now to make it home by midnight.

The one full, meaningful, dinner date that I don't want to run screaming from. Too bad its mere minutes before I must fly back.

But maybe it's the start of something special. Always leave her wanting more, right? Or is it never leave her wanting more? Anyway, you get the idea.

I try and take stock of what just transpired: 6 years of looking. Countless trips back-and-forth. Interminable video calls. Incessant biodata shares. Innumerable dates. Down to 6 prospective matches. Of which 1 remains. I am not superstitious in the slightest, but maybe this one was written in the stars.

I say my goodbye to Ms S, drop her off to her car, and leg it to the Dhaba exit, where lo and behold, Automan is waiting for me.

Headlights on, lawn-mower engine revving.

"Oho! Banni saar, marriage aaita sir?"

All before I even settle down in the church pew. Indians and cutting to the chase.

"Hello boss! Almost. Can we get to this address fast?"

"No problem saar. Two minutes."

****

"Do one thing, just get off at the bus stop. We'll drive you to the airport.", dad on the blower.

"Are you sure? It's like miles away, and you'll be back home really late!"

"Yeah, it's fine. Don't worry. We are already here anyway."

I wish Automan (and by extension his daughter) good luck, get down, and walk towards my dad's car.

"We'll be fine, relax guys. Plenty of time.", I say.

"Yeah, there won't be any traffic anyway.", mom says.

"Well, how was she?", mom asks.

Too good to be true, would be an apt response.

"She was actually perfect."

Total silence in the car as dad ducks and weaves through the traffic. Stray cows, cart pushers, two-wheelers with 4 people on board, lorries with one headlight. The usual.

"Are you serious?", dad finally breaks the silence.

"Yeah…"

"Are you sure?", mom asks.

I mean, how can I be sure? I spent couple of hours with her. But I know there's plenty there to like.

"Yes…"

"Wow! And does she like you too?", dad with a touch of astonishment in his voice.

"I guess so. She definitely likes Ireland…"

"Maybe she's just saying yes to you so she can live in Ireland. You should have told her you plan on moving back to India.", mom the shrewd negotiator.

"Mom, it's fine. I don't think it's that."

"Okay, and is she okay with leaving her job and all?"

"Yeah, she's not too fussed about it."

"That's good. And she's not a Vegan or whatever right?"

"No…"

"And she doesn't think its unnatural to have children?"

"No…"

"We've been looking for so long, I find it hard to believe that it could be done now.", my mom says.

"Think it's too good to be true?", I ask.

Moms know best, remember?

"Maybe, let's see."

"So, what next?", I ask.

"What do you mean?", dad says.

"Like, what's the next step in the process. Now that we like each other…"

"You don't worry about all that, you won't understand it anyway.", mom says. "You just keep in touch with her and see how things go, video calls and all that. And be sure that she's the one!"

"Okay…"

My phone buzzes. WhatsApp from Ms S. Battery's nearly dead, and I need to stream the Arsenal match after check-in. Better hope I find a charger. I look at the preview anyway:

"Thanks for a nice evening. Just reach…."

Okay, she's made it home safe and sound then.

More ducking and weaving in traffic. We are whizzing past the brand-new-and-almost empty apartments by the airport now. The road is as chock-a-block as ever. Nearly there. And it's almost midnight.

"You sure you took your passport?", dad asks this time. 97th time.

"Yes. All set."

"Okay great."

We pull into the parking lot bang on midnight. I jump out, pop the boot, and grab my bag. We walk towards the "Departures" area.

I hug my mom goodbye, shake hands with my dad, nod at the policeman diligently checking passports, and enter the airport through the huge glass doors.

Whew. The last few minutes of my rapid holiday.

My parents are on the other side of the glass, waving goodbye. I take my phone out to make my customary call to them as I walk past security. Glance at my dwindling

battery and decide to send a quick response to Ms S'
WhatsApp first. Open it. It reads:

*"Thanks for a nice evening. Just reached home and had a
chat with my parents. I think we have a great connection,
but if your birth-time on your profile is correct, we can't
move ahead because we have a low Kundli match. Shame!
Good luck on your search."*

Ah yes. Of course, this was written in the bloody stars.

I am half-tempted to send a thumbs-up emoji, but flick
back to the main screen and dial my dad's number instead.
He answers on the first ring because he knows I'd call.
Mom and dad are still waving.

"Hi, all good?"

"Yeah...it's just that..."

"Take care and have a nice flight beta, message us when
you land!", mom yelling in the background.

"Yes, I will…it's just that there's no point in taking things forward with her…"

"Oh? Why not?"

"Apparently the ku…"

And then my phone dies.

So, I mime "because we have a low-Kundli match" through the glass panes at my parents.

I can feel the stoic policeman eyeing me up. I probably looked like a budget SRK in that song from Swades. I was pointing at the sky, making twinkling gestures with my hand (stars), running my fingers across my neck (dead), and pointing my thumbs down. My dad, a Physicist, probably thinks I am referring to a Supernova. My mom is certain that her firstborn has gone full retard. My parents just stand there, transfixed, on the other side of the glass. Watching their 35-year-old son about to get arrested by an equally confused policeman.

••

I didn't get arrested. But I did get delayed in clearing security. Which means my phone remained dead. Along with my boarding passes. A bit of argy-bargy with the customer care rep, and I was finally in the gate just as my name was called on the Tannoy for "Last and final request to board..."

I turned around towards the general direction of Bangalore for yet another goodbye. It was at least an eventful trip.

New perspectives, old failings, crap roads, pretty women, amazing food.

I am sure I'll be back soon.

Epilogue

The less than smooth landing woke me up.

I slept the entire journey. All 13 hours of it. It was a pitch-dark and warm 3AM when I shut my eyes. And a freezing but bright 12PM as we taxied in Dublin.

I autopiloted through security and customs. Waited for the always late park-and-ride bus to the airport parking lot. Jogged the last few metres to my frozen-solid car. And realised I had left my car keys back in Bangalore.

Moms know best.

So, I borrow a sweet old-lady's phone to Google the dealership's number. Who thanks to capitalism, my apparent religion, is quite obviously shut on a Sunday morning.

Which means my only way home is to get over my hatred of public transport and bus-it.

Nobody on it thankfully. I lie down in the last row. Shoes on the seat. Screw it. I had metaphorically squeezed into my LBD, and still come up short.

It's just...the world we live in now.

Our experiences, beliefs, wants...aren't really ours to begin with. They are moulded, shaped, stroked by innumerable things outside our control. Why do I believe what I believe? Why do I want what I want?

To have two consenting adult, strangers each with their own worldview, to agree on the small matter of spending their lives together with total glee is perhaps stretching it a tad. It can be done, of course, and it happens in droves every day everywhere on earth.

But nobody said it'd be easy. And it isn't getting easier.

But who wants easy anyway?

I know what I want. I know what needs to happen for me to get it. I am willing to put in the work to make it happen. Success then, at least in this context, is simply a matter of time. And I have plenty of that. What else do I have going on in my life anyway?

Blow it up and start over.

Back to the drawing board, fresh long-list, shorter-shortlist, more trips back-and-forth, more questions, more information, more disappointments.

But I still need just the one to go my way.

Go big or go home, right?

THE END

About the Author

Akarsh Nalawade continues to survive and thrive in Ireland. Between the Arsenal, writing, trips to Bengaluru, and shitposting, he harbours a lifelong dream of eventually completing an Oscar-winning screenplay. You can block him on Twitter @akarshnalawade.

Printed in Great Britain
by Amazon

16761082R00091